SAVES THE DAY

Georgiana
Deutsch

Vicki
Gausden

Kane Miller
A DIVISION OF EDC PUBLISHING

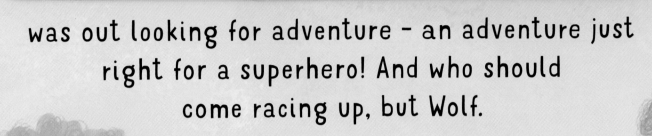

was out looking for adventure – an adventure just right for a superhero! And who should come racing up, but Wolf.

"Help!" Wolf squealed, tail trembling and whiskers quivering. "Something is making a terrible noise in the Dark Forest! It might be a MONSTER!"

leapt high into the air. "At last! This is my chance to be a REAL SUPERHERO. Don't worry, Wolf. You'll be safe with me."

Let's GO!

"Wait for me!" Wolf panted, struggling to keep up as they dashed to the Dark Forest at superhero speed.

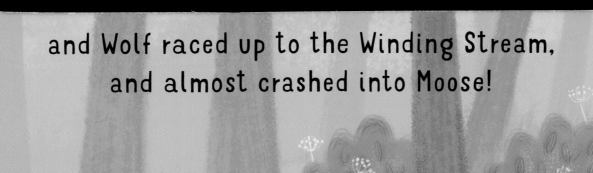

and Wolf raced up to the Winding Stream,
and almost crashed into Moose!

"There's something
scary in the Dark Forest!"
gulped Moose. "I heard
such a strange SNUFFLING
noise. I hope it's not
a scary monster!"

Just then, there was a rustling
in the trees ...

...and Owl came flapping over.
"Eeek!" she screeched. "I heard an awful GROAN
from the Very Tall Tree!"
"Oh no!" shivered Moose. "It really IS a monster!
Whatever will we do?"

gathered the animals together. "Don't panic, everyone! There's nothing too big or too scary for this superhero. We must go to the Very Tall Tree."

The animals tiptoed with superhero stealth over the Rickety Bridge.

█████████████████

carried them with superhero strength through
the Squelchy Bog . . .

...and there, ahead of them, was the Very Tall Tree. They heard a CREAK! CREAK! GROAN! from high up in the tallest branches.

"I'm scared!" shivered Moose. "Me too!" whispered Wolf.

wasn't afraid – not one bit. "I'll go and investigate.
Stay here and don't make a sound!"
But suddenly, a strange SQUEAL rang through the air.

Wolf huddled behind Owl who hid
behind Moose as the noises got
louder...

SCUFFLE!

SCRAMBLE!

"HELP!"

peered up into the branches using extra-strong superhero vision, and gasped. Right at the top of the tree, clinging on to the branches, was Hare!

"Help!" squealed Hare. "I climbed too high and now I can't get down. I thought no one would ever find me!"

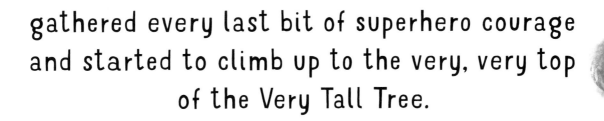

gathered every last bit of superhero courage and started to climb up to the very, very top of the Very Tall Tree.

Don't worry, Hare! I'm coming to rescue you!

"It's so high!" squeaked Wolf.
"I can't look!"
"Me neither!" cried Moose.
"Owl, YOU look!"

But by the time
the animals peeped out
from behind the rock ...

...the rescue mission was complete!

"Thank you so much!" gasped Hare. "You saved me!"
"You're the bravest superhero ever!" cheered Owl.

was so happy to have saved the day.

It's what superheroes do!

And as the sun set over the Dark Forest,
the friends all agreed that they couldn't wait
for their next adventure.

Add a name to be the star of this story!

★

Carefully remove the letters you need from the transparent
sticker sheet by pushing from the reverse side.

★

Make sure the name is placed in the center of the shiny oblong shape
on the opposite page.

★

The stickers may be removed and reused.